THE AMAZING ADVENTURES OF SUPERMAN!

Day of the Bizarros!

by Benjamin Bird

illustrated by Tim Levins

Superman created by Jerry Siegel and Joe Shuster
by special arrangement with the Jerry Siegel family

PICTURE WINDOW BOOKS
a capstone imprint

The Amazing Adventures of Superman
is published by Picture Window Books
a Capstone Imprint
1710 Roe Crest Drive
North Mankato, Minnesota 56003
www.capstonepub.com

STAR34620

Cataloging-in-Publication Data is available at the Library of Congress website.
ISBN: 978-1-4795-6518-4 (library binding)
ISBN: 978-1-4795-6522-1 (paperback)
ISBN: 978-1-4795-8458-1 (eBook)

Summary: While BATMAN is away, SUPERMAN protects Gotham City. But when BIZARRO
SUPERMAN and BIZARRO KRYPTO come to help the MAN OF STEEL, they want to right all
wrongs — but instead, they wrong all rights! Now the Joker is on the loose, and the city is
in chaos. The heroes will have to put an end to the . . . Day of the Bizarros!

Designer: Bob Lentz

Printed in the United States of America in North Mankato, Minnesota.
042015   008823CGF15

TABLE OF CONTENTS

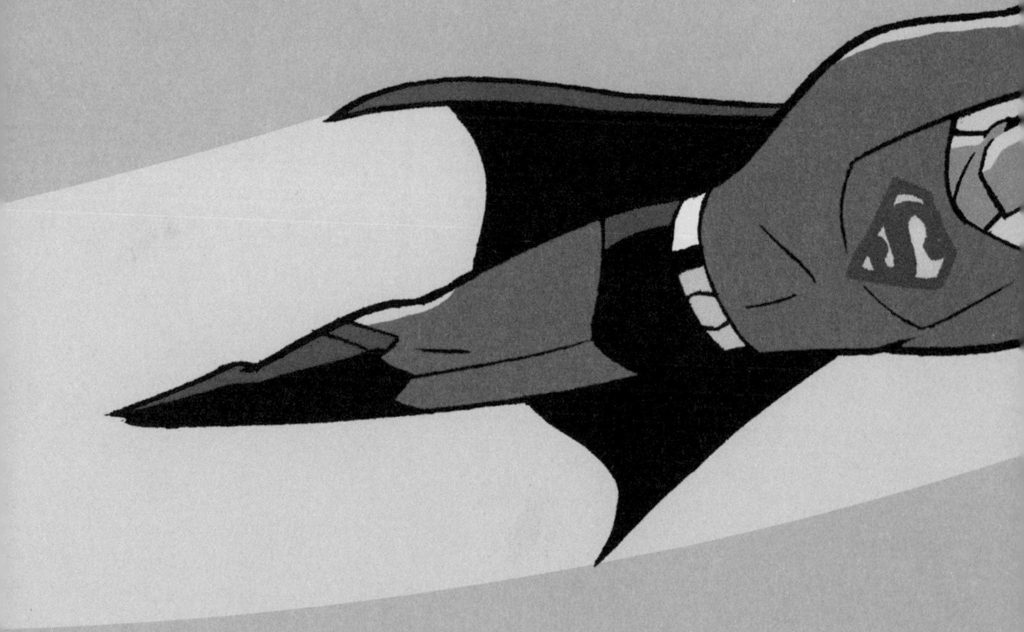

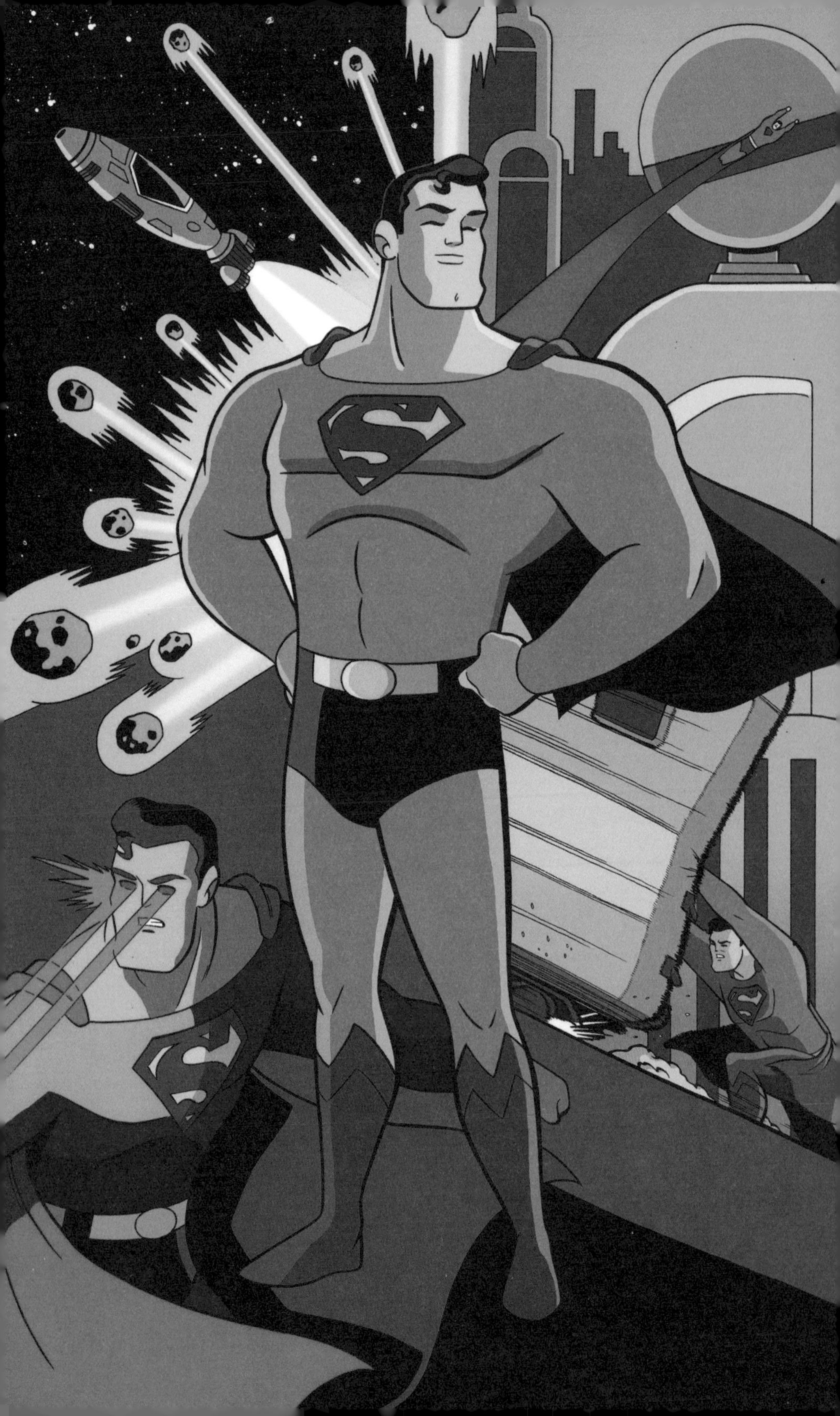

Born among the stars.

Raised on planet Earth.

With incredible powers,

he became the

World's Greatest Super Hero.

These are...

THE AMAZING ADVENTURES OF SUPERMAN!

Chapter 1

FUNNY BUSINESS

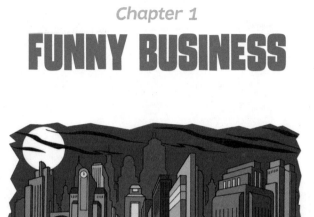

Superman soars high

above Gotham City. While

Batman is away, the Man of

Steel protects his friend's

hometown.

Superman's loyal dog
follows closely behind.
Krypto barks as the super
heroes fly over the city's
prison. BARK! BARK!

"Don't worry, old pal,"
says Superman. "The Joker
is locked safely inside.
We won't have any funny
business tonight."

Meanwhile, a somewhat familiar face looks on from Bizarro World. This distant, square-shaped planet is the opposite of Earth. Its heroes are the opposite, too.

"Criminals no belong in prison," says Bizarro. "Us help Superman wrong his rights."

"Bark!" agrees his not-so-loyal dog, Bizarro Krypto.

* * *

A short time later, the backward duo lands on Earth. Their spaceship crashes into a prison. Criminals escape through the damaged walls.

Bizarro and his dog exit

the ship. "Me land perfectly

terrible!" Bizarro smiles.

"Thanks!" shouts the

Joker, fleeing the prison.

"Us just doing what is wrong," Bizarro explains, "which is always right!"

"HA!" The Joker laughs. "I like the way you think."

FIZZ! BANG! Bizarro's spaceship begins to spark.

"Need a ride?" the Joker asks the backward heroes.

They shake their heads.

"I'll take that as a yes," says the villain.

Chapter 2

WRONGING RIGHTS

High above the city,

Krypto hears trouble with his

super-hearing. He alerts his

master.

With his super-vision,

Superman spots the Joker.

The villain barrels through the streets below inside his Jokermobile.

Superman notices the passengers. "Bizarro," he says, "and Bizarro Krypto!"

The super heroes dive from the sky like missiles.

"What are you doing?" Superman asks his backward double.

"Us turn ugly new buildings into beautiful ruins!" Bizarro explains.

The Joker parks the Jokermobile in front of the Gotham City Bank.

He presses a red button

on the vehicle's control

panel. **BEEP!** A giant boxing

glove appears from beneath

the Jokermobile's hood.

It blasts toward the bank.

 The glove

smashes through the bank

wall and into the vault.

Money spills onto the

street. Prisoners flock to the

cash like hungry birds.

"Freeze!" Superman tells

the crooks.

Krypto hears this word

and blasts the crooks with

his freeze breath. FWOOSH!

They turn into icy statues.

People on the street
cheer for the super heroes.
"Listen to them
cheering," grumbles Bizarro.
"They not like Superman.
Me must stop him!"

Chapter 3

HORRIBLE ADVENTURE

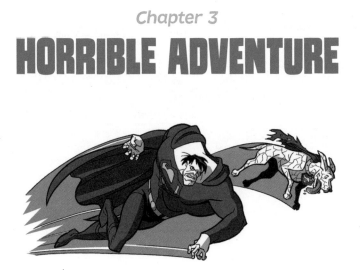

 Bizarro and his dog crash through the roof of the Jokermobile.

"My car!" cries the Joker.

"You welcome," Bizarro says, soaring into the sky.

The backward hero and

his not-so-loyal hound

streak toward Superman.

Superman thinks fast.

"Stop!" he shouts. "Look!"

The Man of Steel points

at the damaged city below.

"Look at all the good work the Joker has done," Superman says. "Doesn't he deserve a reward?"

The backward heroes shake their heads yes.

Moments later, Bizarro arrives at the prison with an armful of icy crooks. Once inside, he thaws them with his flame breath.

"Prison the best reward of all," Bizarro says.

Bizarro Krypto arrives
soon after, with the Joker in
his super-strong jaws.

With the prisoners back
in their cells, the super
heroes fix the prison walls.

Then Bizarro points to his steaming spaceship.

"I know someone who can fix that too," Superman says.

Just then, that someone arrives in the Batmobile. "What happened here?" asks Batman.

Superman smiles. "Just another amazing — I mean, HORRIBLE adventure!"

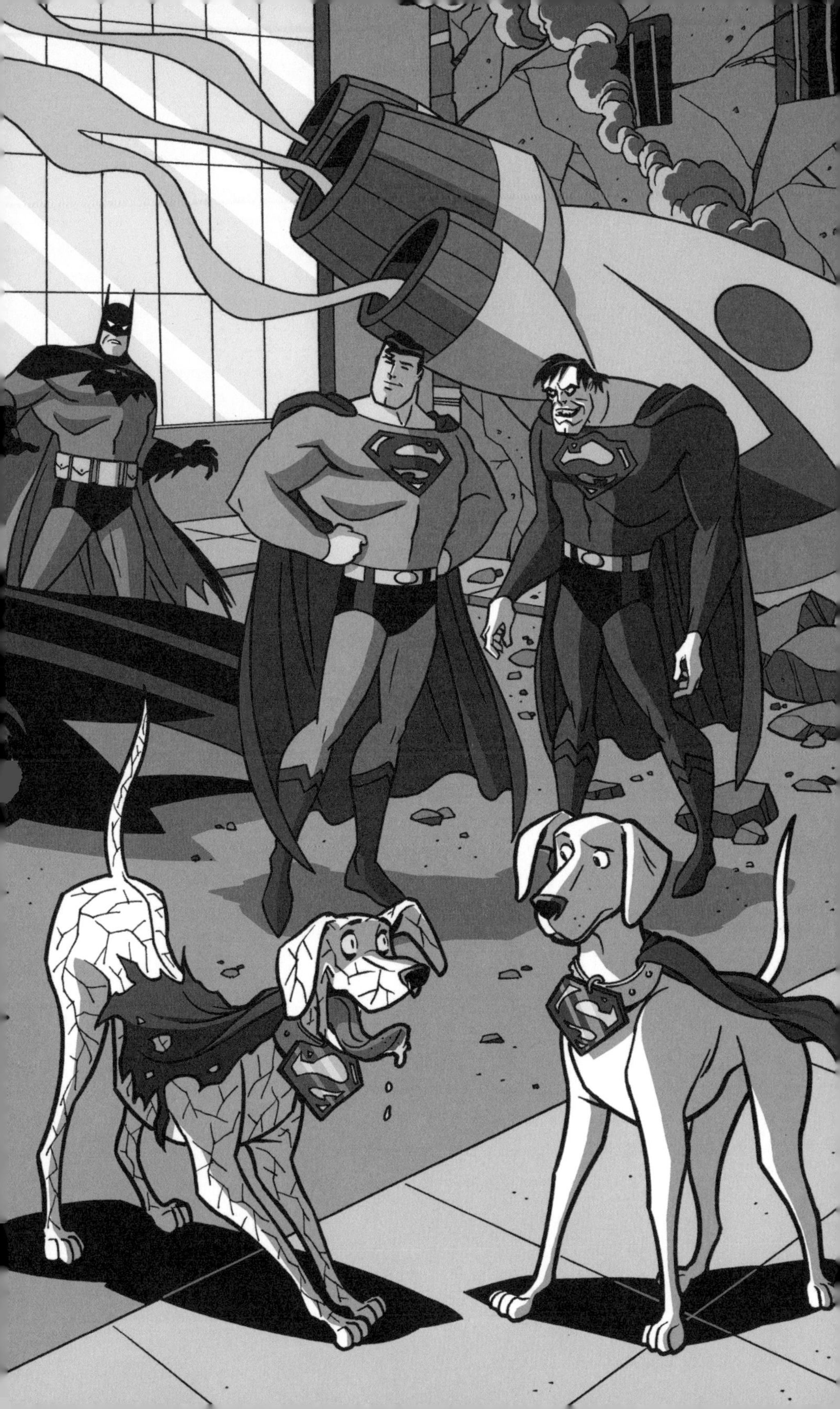

SUPERMAN'S
SECRET MESSAGE!

Hey, kids! What's the opposite
of working alone?

Use the code
below to solve the
secret message!

loyal (LOI-uhl) — firm in supporting or faithful to another

opposite (OP-uh-zit) — completely different

reward (ri-WORD) — something you receive for doing something good

ruins (ROO-ins) — the remains of something that has collapsed or been destroyed

vault (VAWLT) — a room at a bank used for keeping money or other valuables

villain (VIL-uhn) — an evil person

Battle of the Super Heroes!

Escape from Future World!

Alien Superman!

Creatures from Planet X!